GW00870043

Tom
and the
Giant

Will Coleman

Once upon a time Cornwall was ruled by giants.

And the biggest and the hairiest and the ugliest of all the old Cornish giants was called 'DENBRAS' – he was all hairy belly and horrible head.

He lived up on Towednack Hill and thought nothing of snatching a cow or two, **gobble, gobble,** half a dozen sheep, **chomp, chomp,** and a couple of little boys and girls, **clunk, clunk,** before breakfast.

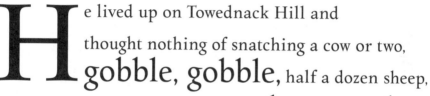

One morning, seeing the great granite boulders scattered across the hillside, he thought to tidy up a bit, and taking the boulders grunt, heave, he built himself heave, grunt, a mighty grunt, heave, grunt, giant's hedge phew... all the way around his hill and down to the sea.

And when he was done he roared,

'I am the King of this castle, and no dirty little rascal may come in here...

...without my say so!"

And he turned and stomped back up the hill to his castle,

STOMP, STOMP,
STOMP.

In the castle-ring was a woman,

"Wife!" roared Denbras, "Fetch me beer!"

and she had to run around and do whatever the giant told her.

She brought him the beer, glug, glug, glug, gurgle, gurgle, belch!

When he had drunk the beer, tired after his morning's work, he lay down for a little shut-eye.

Soon the giant's snores were echoing over the valleys.

Now, down in Bowjeyheer, lived a young man named Tom.

Tom was just making his way home from work when what should he find blocking his road but **the Giant's Hedge?**

"This ent never right!" says Tom. "This road do belong to go straight through here and I shall make sure it does too!"

So, he put his shoulder to that hedge and gave it the most tremendous great shove, **bang, crash, boom, wham, thunk, tinkle, tinkle,** the hedge came down and Tom walked on down the road singing to himself:

"T'was down in Albert Square, I never shall forget…"

Tom's song trickled into the ears of the sleeping Denbras.

"Her eyes they shone like diamonds..."

One great hairy eye opened.

"...and the evening it was..."

Two great hairy eyes opened.

"...wet, wet, wet..."

The giant gave a great hairy yawn, yaaar, got his great hairy belly out of bed, flub-a-dub, got his great hairy legs out of bed, thomp-a-stomp, stretched his great hairy arms, crick-a-crack, and stood himself up to look out over his country.

There, skipping down the road, merry as a skylark, was young Tom!

"**Oy,** you impudent little scrub, whadever do 'ee mean coming in here disturbing my rest?" shouted old Denbras.

"**I,**" says Tom, "am on the road, and not you nor nobody twice your size is going to put me off it. So you may keep your breath to cool your porridge!"

"What!" bellowed Denbras, "you saucy young whelp. I'll drive 'ee out of here quicker than you came in!"

"Don't ee crow too soon, my old cock," says Tom, "for I ent afeared of ee!"

You see, what Denbras didn't know was that Tom was the finest wrestler in the whole of Cornwall.

"With one blow of my fist," roared the giant, "I'll scat your miserable little brains out!"

But, as the huge hairy fist came whistling through the air towards him, Tom grabbed hold of the giant's wrist and, with a well-timed tug, catches him off balance.

The giant toppled onto his stomach with a mighty CRASH!

"Come on," says Tom, "that was far too easy. Let's have another hitch!"

"Ohhhh, my poor belly," groaned Denbras, staggering to his feet. "I'll kick the little blighter from here to the moon!"

But, as the great hairy boot came screaming through the air towards him, Tom **grabbed** hold of the giant's ankle and, with a well-timed boot to his other shin, catches the giant off balance a second time.

The giant toppled onto his back with another almighty CRASH!

"**Come on,**" says Tom, "I heard you was a bit of a hard nut. Lets have another hitch".

Now the giant got up very slowly.

"Oh, my poor insides... **oh,** my poor outsides... **oh,** my poor backsides..."

Denbras puffed himself up to his full height, let out a **mighty yell** and charged at Tom, waving his arms and rolling his eyes.

Tom wasn't impressed by all that hot air.

He just leapt up, grabbed the giant by his jacket,
pulled him down and put him on his back!
The giant fell across a sharp rock.

Tom heard his back bone go... **crrrrack...!**

My, how that giant **hollered** and **howled!**

"**Hush thy bleating,**" called Tom. "I'll plug your wound with a bit of turf and you'll be as right as rain to once."

And Tom began kicking up grass and earth

and shoving it into the giant's wound

to stop the bleeding.

"Tis no use, Tom," croaked Denbras, "I fear I shall kick the bucket; you have killed me! But... before I die... with my final breath...

I shall do you a favour. For I do like you, for your fair play and courage, gwary wheag yu gwary teague, as they say in the Old Language.

Up in my castle there's silver; you can have it. There's gold; 'tis all for you. There's tin ore just waiting to be dressed, enough to last you a lifetime. You are a rich man Tom, yorra ichem ant ommy, yobba richul mabble Tobble. Yop!"

And he was dead.

What's the first thing Tom did?

He piled green oak branches, stones
and earth over the giant's dead body;
raised a barrow over him to give him a
decent burial (still see it there to this day).

Then?

Off up to the castle, and what did Tom find?

"Silver! I can have it!" says Tom.

"Gold! 'Tis all for me!" says Tom.

"Tin ore, just waiting to be dressed! Enough to last me a lifetime!" says Tom.

"I'm a rich man!"

But there in the castle-ring was the finest-looking woman Tom had ever seen.

"Hullo," she says, "who are you?"

"I'm Tom," says Tom, "who are you?"

"I'm Joan," says Joan, "where's my husband, Denbras, the giant?"

"Husband? Oh heng! Well, er, I've slightly, er, killed him!" gulps Tom.

"Killed him? You never did!"

"Did too!"

"Thank you Tom!" says Joan.

"Thank you? For killing your husband?"

"Yes, don't you see? Now the Giant's dead; all this silver! I can have it!" says Joan. "All this gold! 'Tis all for me!" says Joan. "All this tin ore, just waiting to be dressed. Enough to last me a lifetime!" says Joan.

"Thank you Tom, you have made me a very wealthy woman," and she shook him firmly by the hand.

"Oh, that's all right, don't mention it," muttered Tom weakly,
and turned to leave.

Just as Tom had dragged his footsteps as
far as the castle-ring, Joan called after him,

"Tom, I been thinking.
I shall be needing a new husband;
are 'ee interested?"

Tom was some interested sure enough and he was back by Joan's side in a twinkling.

They very quickly agreed to set the wedding date for Golowan (midsummer's eve) and piled up branches and wood to create the biggest hill-top bonfire ever seen.

Then they invited all Tom's family,

which was large,

and all Joan's family,

which was larger,

and all the people from the neighbouring parishes

(so they wouldn't feel left out) to join them.

And the eating
and the drinking.
and the singing
and the dancing to the piper's
music went on
all night long.

Tom and Joan's descendants keep up the annual feast to this day. So, should you be in Cornwall for Golowan (23rd June) head up to the hilltops and join in the midsummer fun.

Er co Big Dave Reynolds – gean kernuack gweer!
To the memory of Big Dave Reynolds –
a real Cornish Giant!

First published in 2005 by Brave Tales Ltd.
© Brave Tales Ltd.
ISBN 0–9549657–2–8
Illustration by Jago, www.jagoillustration.co.uk
Designed and typeset by Gendall, www.gendall.co.uk

Telephone (01208) 873953
Email admin@bravetales.com
Website www.bravetales.com

Other titles in the series: